1

2

1

0

Sara ... **er** is the author and illustrator of the award-winning
Fiv ... *tle Fiends*. She has never seen a monster but is sure
that they ... exist somewhere and are extremely helpful when baking.
Her favou ... te cake is Lemon Drizzle, but she is keen on biscuits too.
Her other l ... oks for Frances Lincoln are *Batty* and *Monster Day at Work.*

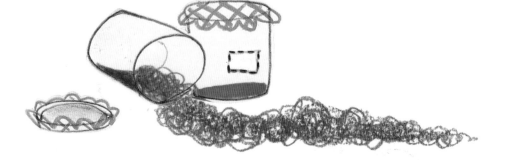

For Great Aunt Mags, as funky as Mrs Muffly -
much loved, and greatly missed

Mrs Muffly's Monster copyright © Frances Lincoln Limited 2008
Text and illustrations copyright © Sarah Dyer 2008

First published in Great Britain and in the USA in 2008 by
Frances Lincoln Children's Books, 4 Torriano Mews,
Torriano Avenue, London NW5 2RZ
www.franceslincoln.com

First paperback published in Great Britain in 2011

A catalogue record for this book is available from the British Library.

ISBN 978-1-84780-040-4

Illustrated with mixed media.

Set in Stone Sans and handlettering

Printed in Dongguan, Guangdong, China by South China Printing in April 2011.

1 3 5 7 9 8 6 4 2

Mrs Muffly's

Monster

Sarah Dyer

F

FRANCES LINCOLN
CHILDREN'S BOOKS

Mrs Muffly lives in a house on top of a hill.
She has always been a bit strange, but lately
she has been acting very, very strangely indeed.
We think that's because she is keeping
a HUGE monster in her house!

This MUST be true because
on Monday
Mrs Muffly went out and
bought a great big pile of sugar.

We think that's because she needs lots of sugar to sweeten him up...

and make him much less scary.

On Tuesday
Mrs Muffly went out and
bought 27 dozen eggs.

We think
that's because
the monster
needs a lot of
eggs to
style his hair
in the morning.

On Wednesday
Mrs Muffly went out and
bought 58 packs of butter.

We think that's because the monster
has the roughest feet in the world.
He needs the butter to soften them up.

On Thursday
Mrs Muffly
went out
and bought
41 sacks
of flour.

We think that's because the monster
uses them as pillows to sleep on at night.
(He's a fussy monster.)

On Friday
Mrs Muffly went out and
bought 464 jars of jam.

We think that's because the monster
loves having really deep jam baths.

On Saturday

Mrs Muffly didn't come out at all.

All that could be seen from her house on the hill

were enormous clouds of smoke, flames

and scary shapes at the windows.

We think the monster must have escaped

and eaten poor Mrs Muffly!

On Sunday
it was the
Giant Cake Competition.
And there, right in the
middle of all the
cakes, was Mrs Muffly
(with not the slightest
sign of being eaten)
with first prize for
the biggest...
MONSTER-SIZED
CAKE EVER!

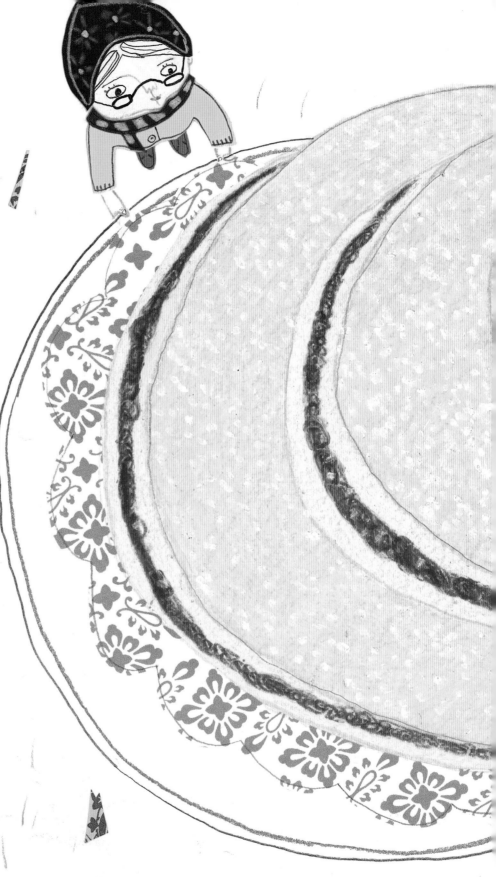

BUT we think

she must have had

some help!

Recipe for a not-quite-so-monster-sized cake

Ingredients

110 g/4 oz/1½ cup butter or margarine

110 g/4 oz/1½ cup caster or superfine sugar

2 medium eggs

110 g/4 oz/ 1 cup self-raising flour

Strawberry jam

Method

1. Heat the oven to 180 C/350 F/Gas 4.
2. Line two 18 cm/7 inch cake tins with baking parchment.
3. Use a hand mixer to cream the butter and the sugar together until pale and fluffy.
4. Beat in the eggs, one by one.
5. Sift the flour and fold in using a large metal spoon.
6. Divide the mixture between the cake tins and gently spread out with a spatula.
7. Bake for 20-25 minutes until golden brown and firm to the touch.
8. Allow the cakes to stand for 5 minutes before turning out on to a wire rack to cool.
9. Sandwich the cakes together with the jam.

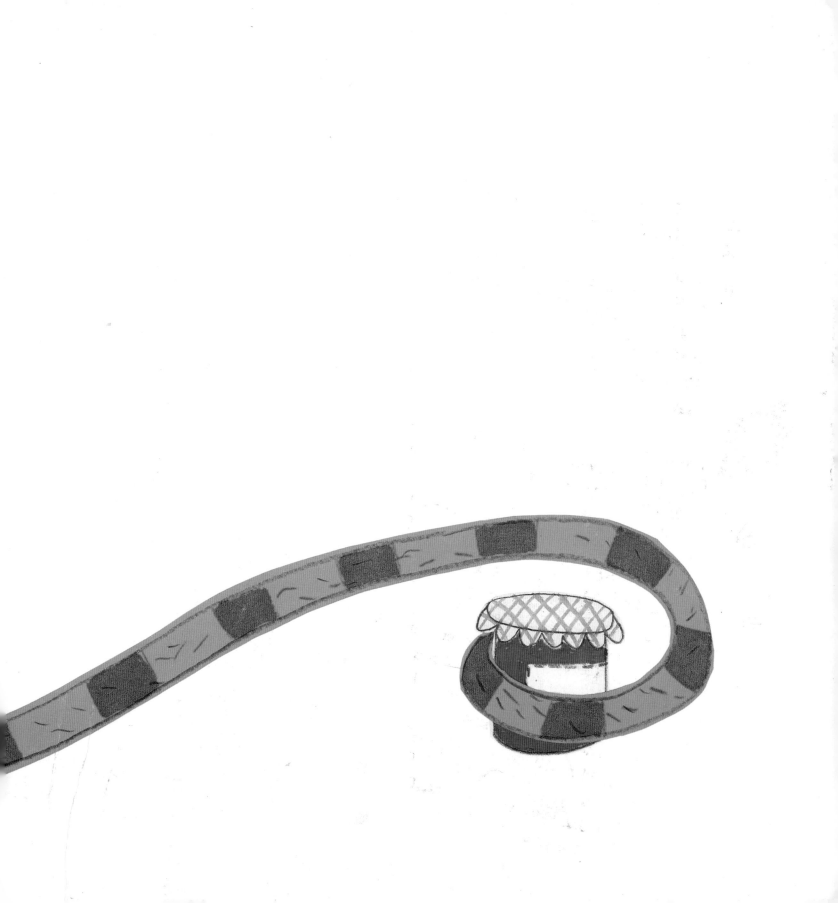

MORE TITLES FROM FRANCES LINCOLN CHILDREN'S BOOKS

Monster Day at Work
Sarah Dyer
Little monster spends a day at work with his father.
First he has to dress and choose which tie to wear.
Then he must travel with Dad and all the other
commuters. At work he eats the biscuits at the
meeting, colours in a graph and even stops off
for a drink on the way home.

Hudson Hates School
Ella Hudson
Hudson loved making things. He liked painting
pictures and building models and baking cakes.
He liked sewing too! But there was one thing
that Hudson really hated . . . and that was school.

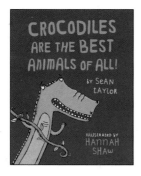

Crocodiles are the Best Animals of All!
Sean Taylor
Illustrated by Hannah Shaw
The animals watch in amazement as Crocodile
demonstrates how he is the best animal of all.
But Donkey knows something that Crocodile
can't do and sets out to prove that donkeys
are best after all.

Frances Lincoln titles are available from all good bookshops.
You can also buy books and find out more about your favourite titles,
authors and illustrators on our website: www.franceslincoln.com